If

Written by Mij Kelly

Illustrated by Mark Beech

If you can keep your head when alligators
are stealing all the bedclothes from your bed
and keep your cool when, 15 minutes later,
a greedy hippo eats your eggy bread …

If you can walk to school with your big brother
although he really is a dreadful sight,
and wave goodbye, although your lovely mother
has turned into a monster overnight ...

If you can cross the playground in the morning –
a playground full of fearsome dinosaurs –
and keep on walking when, without a warning,
they raise their heads and roar and roar and roar …

If you can grin and bear it when your teacher,
who really is a dragon through and through,
tells you to sit beside a toothy creature
who must have just escaped from Scary Zoo ...

If you can lend your ruler – though he chews it –
if you can let him use your felt-tip pens,
if you can lend a hand – although he'll bruise it –
and treat him just like any other friend ...

If you can eat the food served up by mummies
with trolls and lizards in the dinner hall,
and when the others groan and hold their tummies
say, "Actually, that wasn't bad at all ..."

If you can stand and watch a spaceship landing
and when the others run away in fright,
you treat the strange green men with understanding
and though they're rude, you are still polite ...

If you can count to ten while angry rhinos
are grunting (just because they can't do sums)
and say, "I'll teach you everything that I know
but quick – before the dragon teacher comes ..."

And then, if you can play your new recorder
up there, on stage – you're feeling rather stressed
– and all around there's panic and disorder
but still you try to do your very best …

If you can play at baseball with a cheetah
who, fast as lightning, runs from base to base
and even though you know you'll never beat her,
you somehow keep a smile upon your face,

If you can run, though others can run faster,
and cheer the winner, "Hip-hip-hip hooray!"
if you can try to stop a near-disaster,
although you'd really rather walk away ...

If you can keep your head when all about you
are losing theirs and blaming it on you,
if you can let them fight it out without you,
if everyone's a monster, but not you ...

If then you meet a tearful pirate fairy
and kindly help her up from off the ground
and wonder how the world can be this scary
and stop and think ... and turn ... and look around ...

Then you will see that they're just human beings
with hopes and worries much the same as you.
Despite their snatch and grab and disagreeing
there's lots of lovely things they also do.

If you can see all this and never doubt it
(though crocodiles will eat your cheesy snack)
you'll love the world and everything about it
and – what is more – the world will love you back.

Everyone's a monster

We're all human beings

Ideas for reading

Written by Clare Dowdall BA(Ed), MA(Ed)
Lecturer and Primary Literacy Consultant

Learning objectives: read independently and with increasing fluency longer and less familiar texts; draw together ideas and information from across a whole text; explain organizational features of texts, including layout; engage with books through exploring and enacting interpretations; speak with clarity and use appropriate intonation when reading aloud

Curriculum links: Citizenship: Taking part

Interest words: toothy, fearsome, bruise, understanding, stressed, panic, disorder, disaster, tearful, disagreeing

Word count: 514

Resources: ICT

Getting started

- Introduce the book by showing the front cover and read the blurb together. Help children to notice the poetic style.
- Ask children to explain what is happening in the picture in their own words to a partner and predict what the book might be about.
- Explain that this is a new version of a famous poem called "If" by Rudyard Kipling, and that this version has been written for children.

Reading and responding

- Read pp2–3 together aloud emphasizing the poem's rhythm and rhyme and pointing out the repetition of the word *if*. Ask children to join in as you read again.
- Ask children to read pp2–3 with a partner and count how many events there are in each verse. Remind children to look at the pictures to find the scenes mentioned on each page.
- Support children as they read to the end of the poem, helping them to use punctuation to develop expression and to read with rhythm.